This book belongs to:

....

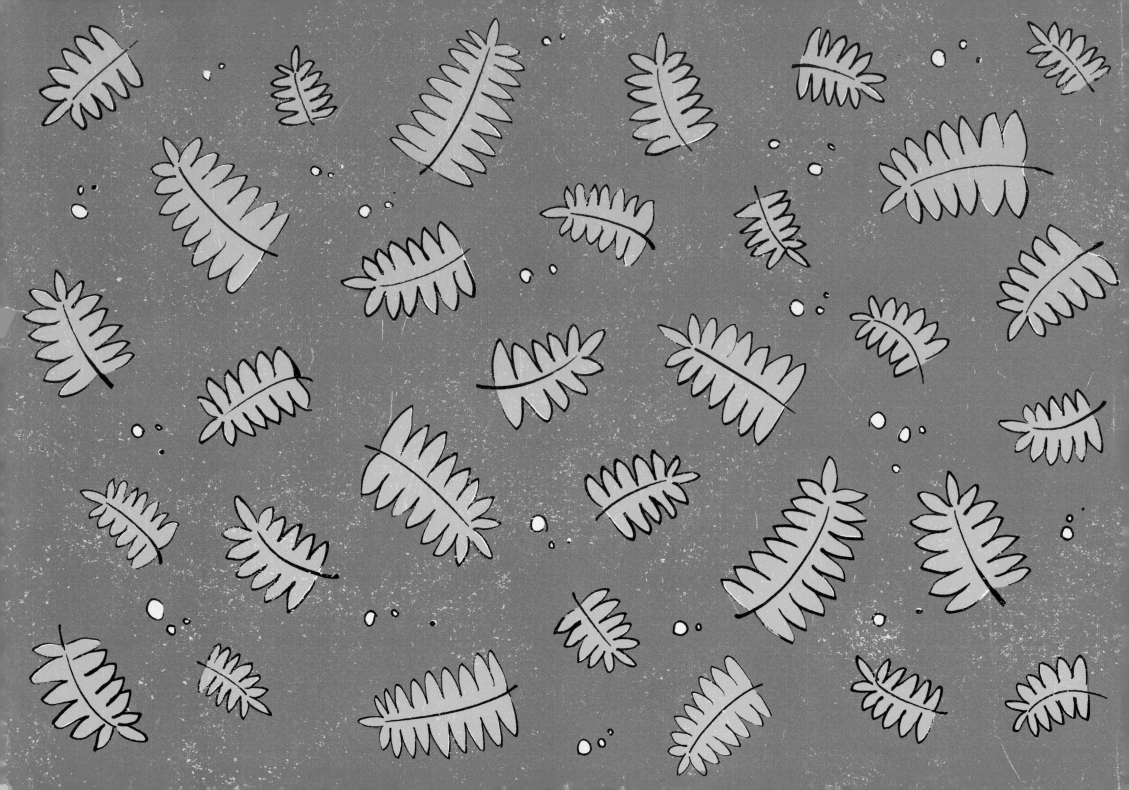

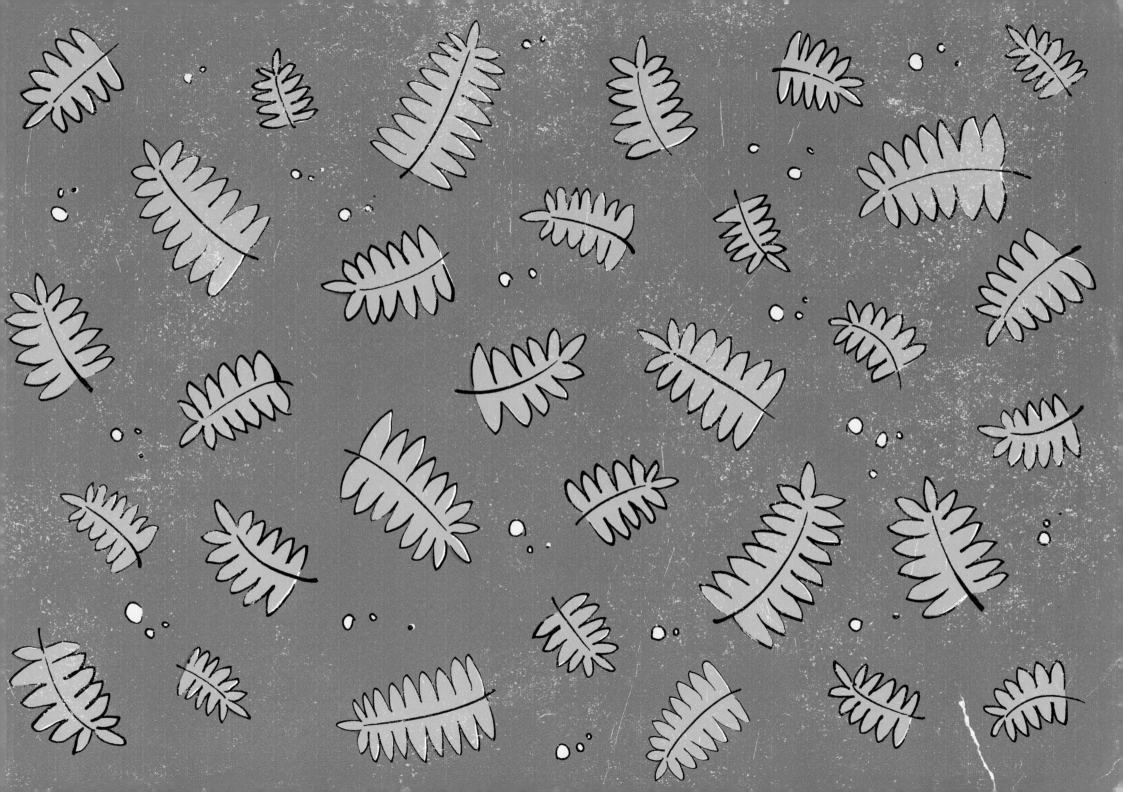

For Frances, who likes jungles.
With love – G.E.

The Big Jungle Mix-Up
First published in hardback in 2012 by Hodder Children's Books
This paperback edition published in 2013

Hodder Children's Books, 338 Euston Road, London, NW1 3BH
Hodder Children's Books Australia, Level 17/207 Kent Street, Sydney, NSW 2000

ISBN: 978 1 444 90305 8

Printed in China

Hodder Children's Books is a division of Hachette Children's Books.
An Hachette UK Company.

www.hachette.co.uk

The Big Jungle Mix-Up

Gareth Edwards
Kanako Usui

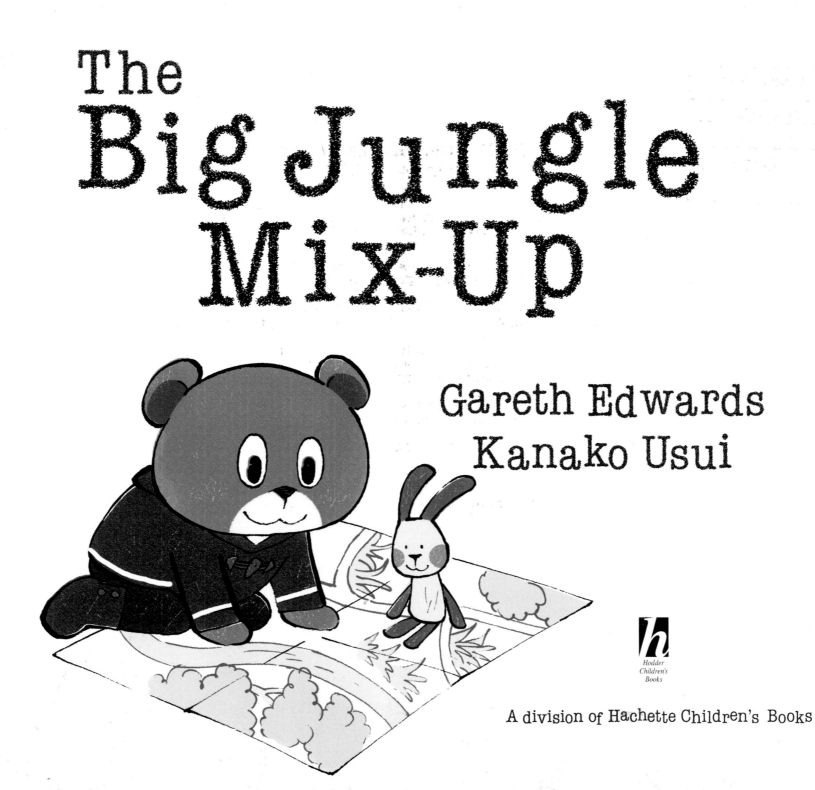

Hodder Children's Books

A division of Hachette Children's Books

"The jungle is deep,
The jungle is wide,
With so many animals
Lurking inside!

I'll tell you about them
As we walk along,
But please say,
Little Bear,
If I get something wrong...

We might find a
monkey,
With feathers and beak!
Pea-green,
carrot-orange.
We'll teach it to
speak!"

"You've got it mixed up!

As orange as a carrot?
A beak that can speak?
Then it must be a...

"I know about parrots –
They've horns on their nose.
They are HUGE
with thick skin
From their head
to their toes."

"You've got it mixed up!

You know **much** less
than I know!

Thick skin and a horn?

Then it **must** be a...

"Oh yes, that's a rhino!
With leathery wings,
And it hangs upside down
Eating mangos and things."

"You've got it mixed up!

Rhinos can't do all that.
If it hangs upside down
Then it **must** be a...

"Of course! That's a **fruit bat**.
They croak, and they **jump**.
They're green and they live
In a bog or a swamp."

"You've got it mixed up!

If it lives in a bog

And it croaks and it jumps,

Then it **must** be a...

"But frogs can be scary.
How fiercely they growl!
Fur peppered with spots
Through the jungle
they prowl."

"You've got it
mixed up!

If its fur is all peppered
With spots, and it growls,
Then it must be a...

"A leopard. You're right!
With its shiny green scales,
And a smile that looks mean
Full of teeth sharp as nails!"

"You've got it
mixed up!

If it has a mean smile
And it's scaly and green,
It's a big...

"A **crocodile!** Help!
Now I'm starting to worry!
It's wearing **red** boots
And its paws are all furry!"

"You've got it mixed up!

There's no croc anywhere!

I'm wearing red boots!

You mean ME,

"There are bears in the jungle?
I had no idea!
Are you scary and fierce?
What's that growling I hear?"

"You've got it mixed up!

I'm as nice as can be! It's my tummy that's growling!

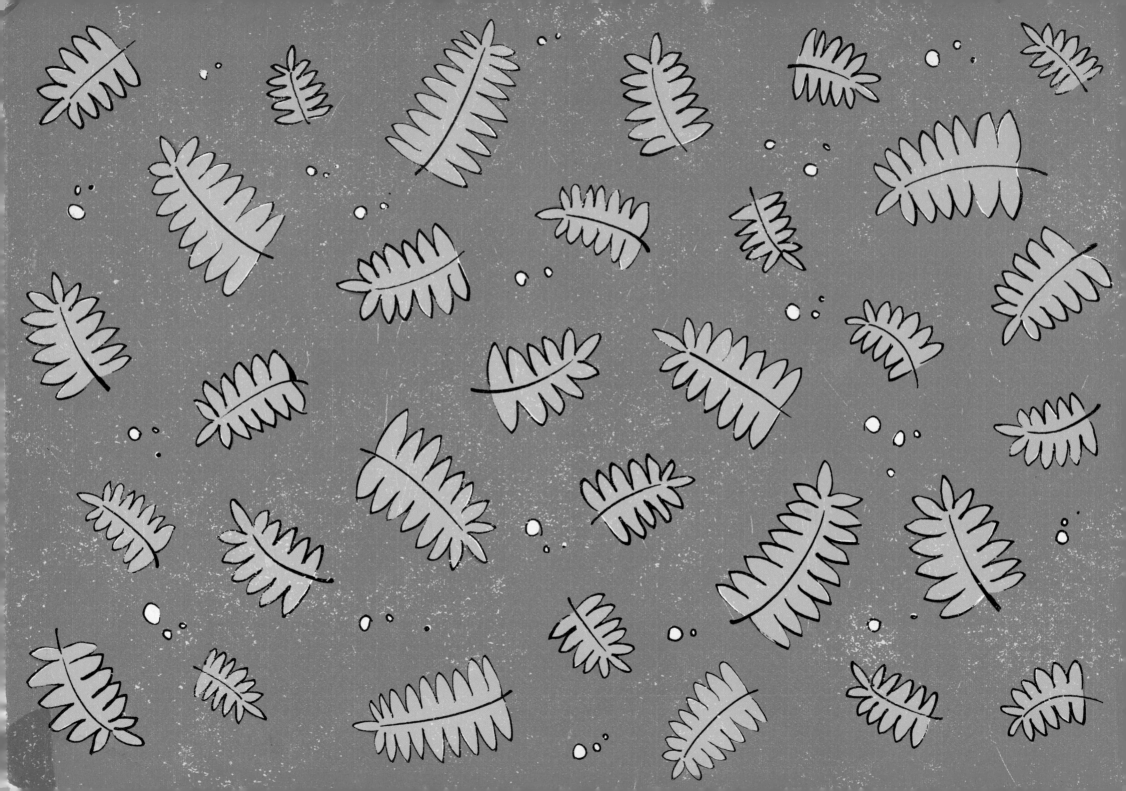

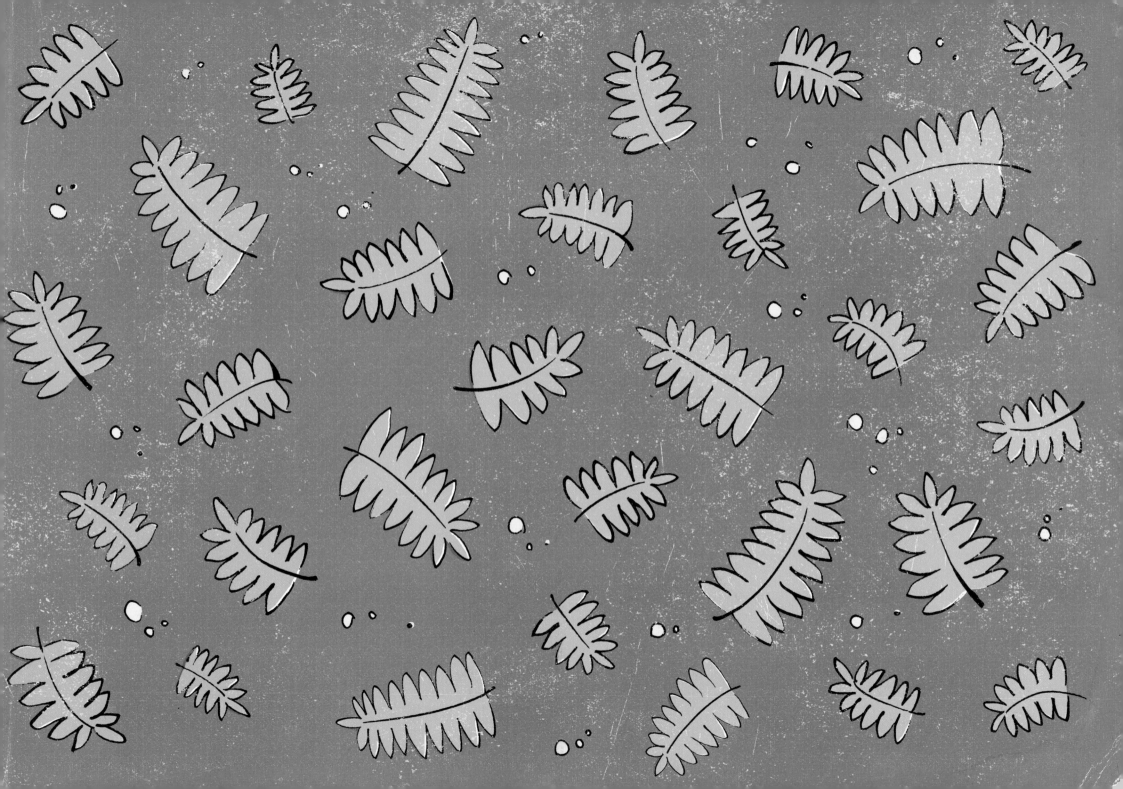

Enjoy more mixed-up fun
with Little Bear:

978 1 444 90305 8

978 0 340 98989 0